Major Glad, Major Dizzy

by Jan Oke with photography by Ian Nolan

Retouching by Tony Swinney
Design by Trudie Burne
Model Making by Bernard Covey
Art Direction by Jan Oke

William and his sister Amelia didn't have many toys and they worked us hard. All day long they lined us up... and knocked us down.

And when
Amelia had to
stop playing to sew
her sampler, William
made us fight
each other.

Even though
we are best
friends!

1870   1880   1890   **1900**   1910   1920   1930   1940   1950   1960   1970   1980   1990   **2000**   2010   the future

We stole food from under
the servant's nose.

I saw that, Major Dizzy.
I've got eyes in the
back of my head
I have.

When trains went past the
whole house rattled and shook.
The walls bulged and the
floorboards shivered.

This is no life for a soldier.
I want to be a hero.

You have jelly on your hat.

One day Amelia was left
alone with us.

I don't want to be a
dainty young lady. I'd
rather watch trains. And if
I can't play with Glad and Dizzy,
I don't think William should
either. It's not fair.

Oh, what a shame! I seem to
have mislaid my needle.
I can't sew now.

Any room for a little 'un?

That head looks
chewy, Wilfred.

I don't believe its paint
would be healthy for
us, Percival.

Under the floor became our own
private empire and we soon
made ourselves comfy.

It is fortunate that our
appearance is so manly,
Major Glad. The mice
are too afraid of
us to attack.

You two are lucky.
I've had my head bitten off.

After a while, no more toys came
to join us.

Little William and Amelia had
vanished and in their place
were grown-ups.

Ho there!
We're bored!
We'd like to come back up now.

When I grow up, I want to be a train driver just like you, Uncle William. Or I want to invent a flying machine or a very fast horseless carriage. Or perhaps I'll be a soldier.

One day, much later, we heard an old man crying. It was William.

Then all was quiet and if we heard music or children's laughter, it sounded a long way off.

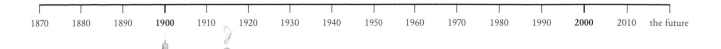

What was that?

Is anyone there?

Have all the children gone away?

Yes. All of them.
All gone away to the country.

PUT THAT LIGHT OUT!

WOOOOOOOOOOOOOOOOOOOOOOOOOOO

WHOMP

WHOMP

WHOMP

ACK-ACK-ACK-ACK-ACK

1870   1880   1890   **1900**   1910   1920   1930   1940   1950   1960   1970   1980   1990   **2000**   2010   the future

Fear not mice!
This may be our finest hour.

We are heroes now, Major Dizzy,
but no one will know of our
bravery this night.

I don't th ink I can

hol d o n much lo ng er.

Goo d bye my fri e nd s.

Our ship of the desert is deserting. Hurry Major! Catch hold of her other leg!

One day, much later, and long after
we had ceased to dream of rescue...

I know that smell! It's jelly
and it's coming from
over here.

MILLY NO! NOT MUM'S KEYS

1870   1880   1890   **1900**   1910   1920   1930   1940   1950   1960   1970   1980   1990   **2000**   2010   the future

It's time we fixed these splintery old floorboards anyway.

Let's have a soft, fluffy carpet!

Look at the toys! And this picture is our house in the olden days. You can take these to show your class Billy.

And I'll help you write a letter to Granny about them. These toys must be even older than her special teddy, Winston. Perhaps they belonged to her grandfather William, who grew up in this house.

There's a dark tunnel. I am definitely the most adventurous bus I know...

Granny will know who Amelia was too. If only these toys could speak. What stories they could tell us about the past   ;-)

To granny,
9, Little Knowle,
Budleigh Salterton,
Devon,
EX9 6QS

Can this really be London? Where are the horses? What are these monstrous contraptions racing past?

Major Glad, I hardly dare open my eyes. All the ladies wear pantaloons! Has the world gone mad? Or have we?

No need for panic, Major Dizzy. We'll be Billy and Milly's toys now. What's the worst that can befall us?